SCHOONER

Written and Illustrated by Pat Lowery Collins

COMMONWEALTH EDITIONS
Beverly, Massachusetts

ISBN 1-889833-35-5

Commonwealth Editions is an imprint of
Memoirs Unlimited, Inc.
21 Lothrop Street,
Beverly, Massachusetts 01915.
Visit us on the Web at
www.commonwealtheditions.com.

Designed by Jill Feron/Feron Design.
Printed in Singapore.

10 9 8 7 6 5 4 3 2 1

For two adventuresome boys,
Nathaniel and Lincoln

Shipbuilding terms in *italics* are
explained in the glossary on page 31.

DECEMBER 23

They're working on something long and skinny in the old shipyard. One end of it points to the sky. One leads down to the river.

I ask one of the men what they're doing.

"We've just laid the *keel*," he says.

"The what?"

"The keel. You might call it the backbone for the *vessel*."

"What kind of vessel?" I ask.

"It's a *schooner*," he says. "It'll look like that picture over there."

The vessel in the painting has all sails blowing. It has two masts that rise high into the air. It rides on calm blue water. It doesn't look as if it started from a keel.

"You'll see," says the man. The other men say he's the owner, and they call him Tom.

"But what's the vessel for?" I want to know.

"Schooners used to be mainly for fishing," Tom says. "This one is for adventure."

DECEMBER 24

They're attaching the *stem,* or front support piece, of the vessel to the keel with a crane. Jim says the stem was first roughed out on the *band saw,* but he uses a tool called an *adze* to make it the right shape.

They use a great big electric saw to mill logs into *planks.* It screeches like fingernails on a blackboard. Tony, the man who runs it, says I can watch if I "steer clear!" There are piles of logs all over the place. The yard dog, Max, runs away whenever Tony turns on the saw.

"It hurts his ears," says Tony. It hurts mine, too.

DECEMBER 25

It's Christmas, and the shipyard is closed. When I go by after dinner, there's a small Christmas tree tied to the stem.

This morning my Dad gave me a model schooner that came in pieces in a box with a chart to tell where each piece goes. My Dad says that Harold, the designer and builder of the real schooner, has the plans for it right in his head. Harold has carved something called a *half-model* that looks exactly like one half of the schooner, but it's much smaller. He leaves it around the shipyard so any of the workers can take a look at it. On the top and flat side you can see the measurements of what are called *stations*. He'll take the vessel's measurements right from this model the way shipbuilders have done for centuries.

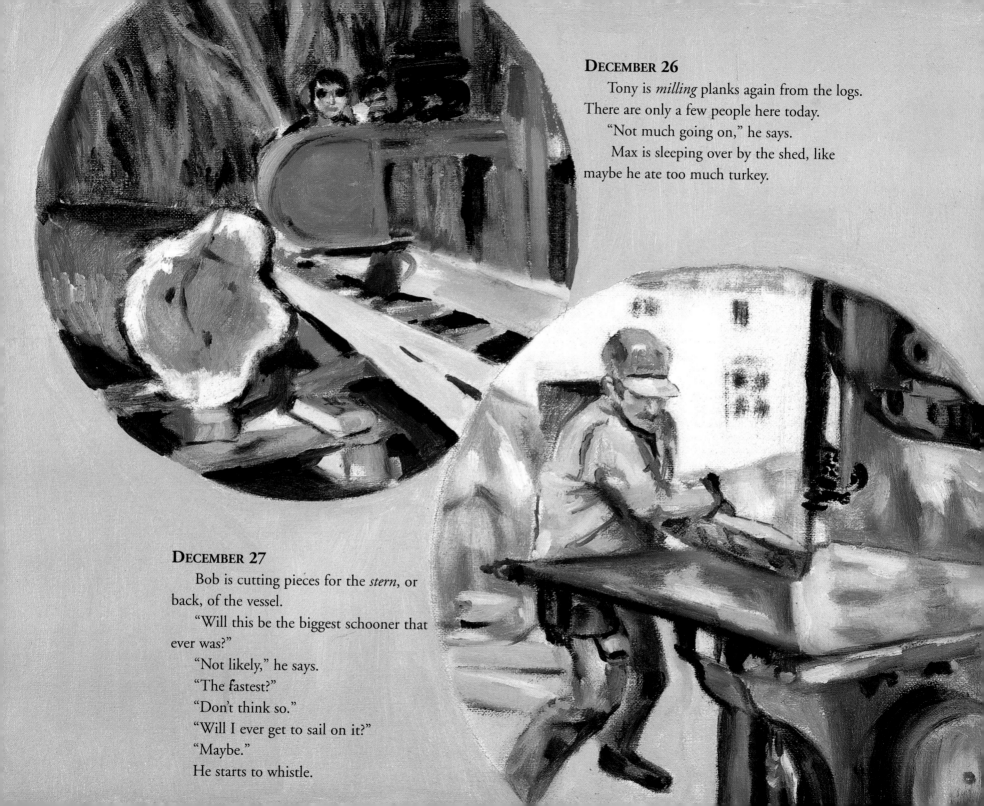

DECEMBER 26

Tony is *milling* planks again from the logs.
There are only a few people here today.

"Not much going on," he says.

Max is sleeping over by the shed, like
maybe he ate too much turkey.

DECEMBER 27

Bob is cutting pieces for the *stern*, or
back, of the vessel.

"Will this be the biggest schooner that
ever was?"

"Not likely," he says.

"The fastest?"

"Don't think so."

"Will I ever get to sail on it?"

"Maybe."

He starts to whistle.

DECEMBER 28

It's Christmas vacation, and Mom has chores for me to do. When I get to the boatyard after lunch, it's busy as a beehive again. The band saw is going.

Dave is putting *graving pieces*, small wooden sections, where there were knots in the wood.

Two older boys are painting the keel with *preservative* paint to keep it from drying out in the sun. The boy named Jeff says the vessel is being made of *green wood*, so they sometimes use linseed oil. He says if I was a little older, maybe I could help, too.

When the *caulking* man comes by I ask, "What do you do?"

"Don't mind him," Jeff tells the man. "He's awful nosy."

"Oh, my job is to keep water out of the *hull*," says the man.

"The what?"

"The body of the vessel."

DECEMBER 29–30

We are going to visit my Aunt Gina. She has a new baby but nobody my age to play with, so it won't be much fun. Babies sleep all the time. I hope I don't miss something important at the shipyard.

"Am I nosy?" I ask my Mom.

"Curious," she says. "You're just very, very curious."

DECEMBER 31

It snowed in the night. I think they won't be working on the vessel today, but there they are again.

"We can't quit," Tom says. "We have a deadline to meet."

Later, my Dad tells me a deadline is an exact time when something has to be finished. "For a vessel," he says, "It has a lot to do with the tides and time of year."

They are fitting the *sternpost* today. It had been resting on the keel, but now they take it off with a big crane, smear tar on it, put it back, and bolt it in place with bolts that are seven feet long. I know that because I asked.

JANUARY 2

Dave is putting preservative paint on the stem.

"When's the deadline?" I ask.

"The middle of June," he says.

He starts to whistle too.

After a while, I go home to work on my own vessel. I am just attaching the stem to the keel when Mom calls me to supper. It's a good thing *I* don't have a deadline.

JANUARY 3

Today they begin to make the *framing stage*, a kind of platform on each side of the keel, where they'll build the *frames* and stand them up. As each new frame is raised, the framing stage moves forward from stern to *bow,* or back to front.

"You'd best stay off of it," Tom tells me.

Tony has been milling more timber and wears earmuffs to cut out the noise. He doesn't like it when I ask to try them on.

JANUARY 10

Everyone is really busy. Jim and Dave are cutting curved pieces of wood called *futtocks* using big pattern molds. These will be put together to become the frames of the vessel. Fran says men used to "beat out," or chop out, the futtocks with a *broadaxe,* but today they use a band saw.

"Each frame will be made of two layers of futtocks," he says, "to give the vessel strength."

Some of the men are already fastening pieces together with funny-looking wooden pins called *trunnels,* or "tree nails." One day I watched them turn these on an electric *lathe.* They use an electric drill to bore the holes for them. "A whole lot easier than in the old days," Peter says, "when the trunnels were made by hand, and you had to use a hand *auger* for each hole."

JANUARY 11

I hear the cry *"Frame Up"* as I park my bike in the mill yard after school. The men are raising the fourth frame and everyone drops what they're doing to come and help. When I do, too, Tom waves me out of the way. Well, just watching is pretty exciting.

"We begin aft," I hear Tom telling a visitor, "And work to the stem."

JANUARY 13

The fifth frame is raised, and I'm beginning to see why they're called ribs. That's just how they look.

JANUARY 15

Every day, now, there's at least one more frame raised. Jim explains how they're called square frames because they have to be placed at right angles or square to the keel.

Jeff has begun to oil the frames with turpentine and linseed oil to keep them from drying out. He says all the wood has to be treated this way.

JANUARY 21

I've been sticking around home for a few afternoons 'cause Mom says I should do school work for a change, and that maybe I'm in the way at the shipyard.

Today I notice a big difference in the vessel. The staging is different, too. There are levels now and ramps up to the highest parts. There are things called *shores* to hold up the frames. But there aren't any railings, and when I first walk up a ramp I almost fall off. Tom yells at me to get down, but I try it again when he isn't looking.

There are lots more frames in place. Tony is milling even bigger logs.

They're putting up a wooden strip called a *ribband*. It's bent into the same shape as the bow, or forward part, of the vessel.

FEBRUARY 4

I understand what the ribband is for when I see how it holds up the forward frames until they're all in place. The half frames at the bow and stern are called *cants*. Jim says they're given a beveled or angled edge so they'll fit tightly. He fastens them with "blind trunnels."

"They're called that," he says, "because you can't get at them from the other side."

FEBRUARY 10

It snowed a few days ago, and I had to go right home after school to shovel and do homework. I'll bet Max misses me.

FEBRUARY 13

Under a tarp, Harold is working on the *horn timber* for the stern, or back, of the vessel. He says it will be held up between heavy *cheeks* timbers attached to the sternposts.

FEBRUARY 20

Harold also chooses the right pieces of wood for each plank. He tells me that later he'll draw a line on the boat, the dubber will cut a flat place with an adze, and Harold will put a wooden strip, or *batten*, on the side of the vessel to make a pattern. They call this *spiling*.

I stop by for just a minute and see that Jim is cutting a groove into the wood where the *garboard,* or first plank, will go. He says the groove is called a *rabbet*. He spells it, "So you won't think it's some long-eared animal that hops."

FEBRUARY 26

They've finished making the box to steam and bend the planks. There is steam coming out of it in big white puffs. The oak garboard is first, and the men are sure happy when they pull it out and hang it. Now Harold can lay the batten on the wood to cut each plank. Dave and Fran keep steaming and fastening. Jim and Peter do the *dubbing* before and the caulking after. Everybody is doing something. They seem to be in a race with each other.

MARCH 3

The planking goes steadily after that. "A *streak* a day is good," says Fran. Tom says how they're "planking upward" from the bottom to the top of the vessel and how all the oak planks below the *waterline* are steamed to fit the ribs. It's like I'm one of the visitors all of a sudden. I don't even have to ask questions

MARCH 13

They're still planking. Harold says the vessel is growing by about a foot every day. Watching it grow is like waiting for my birthday to come.

MARCH 15

There's a big storm and no school for days. Then I
catch chicken pox and have to stay in the house for two
whole weeks. I scratch and sleep a lot and keep telling my
Mom, "I'll bet that vessel will be almost finished when I
get back."

APRIL 1

"Boy! It's way bigger," I say when I see the vessel again.
"Well, of course it is," says Harold. "We've got to meet
that deadline."

I sure am glad they didn't finish it without me.

APRIL 7

More oak is being milled so they can finish planking
to the waterline. From there on up they're using mahogany.

APRIL 17

Jim has been caulking between planks and has left little cotton puffs to mark his work. "You have to do it just right," he says, "a thread to an inch." He tells me how most seams have a thread of cotton on the bottom and a thread of *oakum* on top. He says that oakum is tarred rope fibers with thick paint applied before the seam is puttied. When I ask why, he says, "To make the vessel *watertight*. What did you think?"

"What's watertight?"

"Go ask Tom."

APRIL 22

Fran is coating long oak boards with preservative. He says these will be put on the inside of the frame at the *sheer line*, the place where the deck curves, to hold up the deck beams. He calls them the *clamp* and the *shelf* and says they'll run the whole length of the vessel.

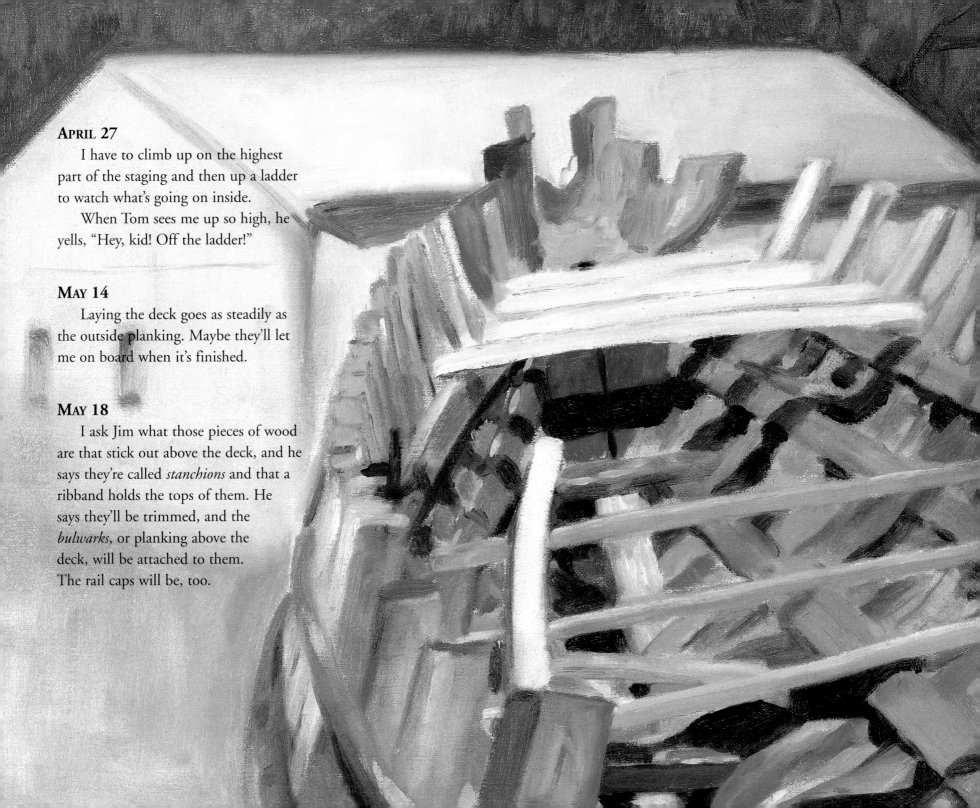

APRIL 27

I have to climb up on the highest part of the staging and then up a ladder to watch what's going on inside.

When Tom sees me up so high, he yells, "Hey, kid! Off the ladder!"

MAY 14

Laying the deck goes as steadily as the outside planking. Maybe they'll let me on board when it's finished.

MAY 18

I ask Jim what those pieces of wood are that stick out above the deck, and he says they're called *stanchions* and that a ribband holds the tops of them. He says they'll be trimmed, and the *bulwarks*, or planking above the deck, will be attached to them. The rail caps will be, too.

MAY 20

They're building some kind of a cabin on the deck.

"Boy would I love to sleep in there!" I tell Tom.

"We won't build the sleeping quarters 'til after the *launching*," he says.

The launching! If I could only be on that vessel for the launching! But it'll never happen. They won't even let me on now, and my Mom would say "no" for sure, anyway.

JUNE 4

It looks like the vessel is being painted red. Jim is putting bronze paint on the bow. When I tell Tom how I don't think I want it to be red, he laughs and says it's just going to be red to the waterline. "And don't ask me where that is. You'll see where the red paint ends." He says the finished vessel above that will be dark green.

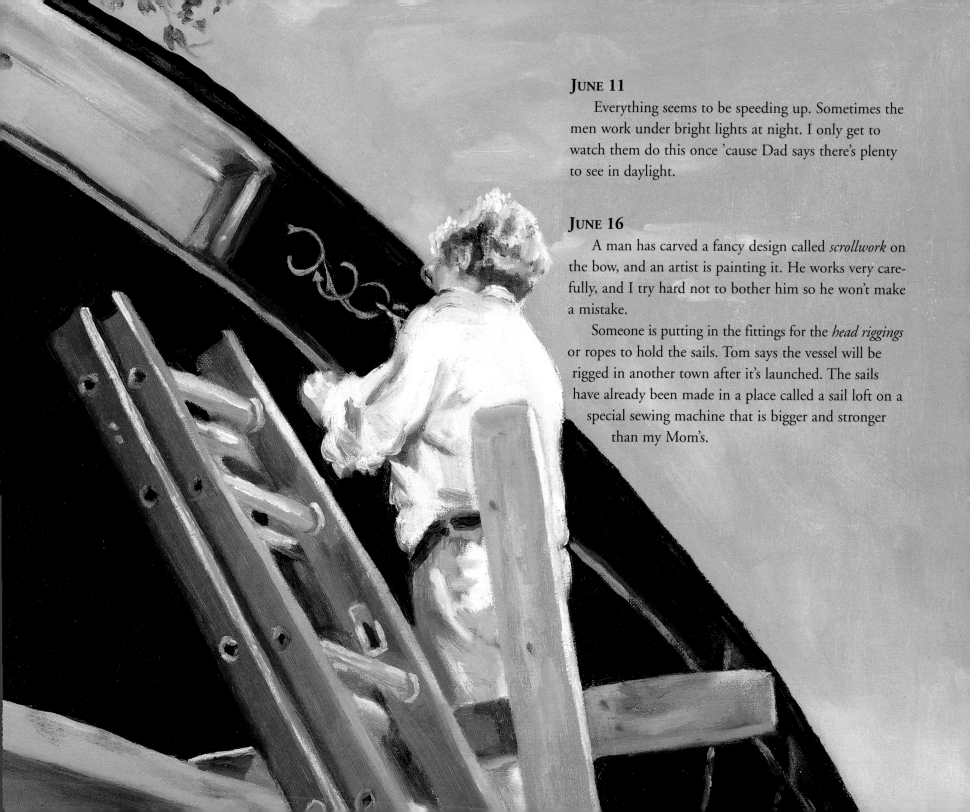

JUNE 11

Everything seems to be speeding up. Sometimes the men work under bright lights at night. I only get to watch them do this once 'cause Dad says there's plenty to see in daylight.

JUNE 16

A man has carved a fancy design called *scrollwork* on the bow, and an artist is painting it. He works very carefully, and I try hard not to bother him so he won't make a mistake.

Someone is putting in the fittings for the *head riggings* or ropes to hold the sails. Tom says the vessel will be rigged in another town after it's launched. The sails have already been made in a place called a sail loft on a special sewing machine that is bigger and stronger than my Mom's.

JUNE 18

People have begun to hurry around the yard as if they can't wait. When I ask Tom if they're going to launch on time he says, "Hope so," but he doesn't say a thing about my coming along.

JUNE 19

"You should have spoken up before this," says my Dad.

"I don't think it's safe," says Mom. "You're not such a great swimmer."

"I'll wear a life jacket."

"It sounds like a once-in-a-lifetime thing," says my Dad.

"You're right," says my Mom.

She's actually agreeing with him!

"But it still seems pretty dangerous to me," she says then. "They haven't launched a vessel like this in fifty years!"

JUNE 20

I hang around all afternoon watching the guys do last-minute things.

I tell Tom, "I'll bet it will be a thrill of a lifetime when you finally launch her."

"You bet," says Tom.

I tell Harold, "This vessel must be the tightest one in the whole world."

"That's what we aim for," he says.

JUNE 21

They're going to launch her right before midnight when the tide is high. Mom lets me stay up. I can't eat supper thinking about it. I wonder what it will be like when she hits the water and if they really will launch her on her side, off greased wooden wedges, like I've heard.

There are people all over the vessel. A lot of them are getting off, now, and coming down the ladder. I sure wish I was up there, but it's too late now. Watching it being built, that was the best thing in the world. There couldn't be anything better than that.

"Hey," yells Tom.

"I think he's calling you," says Mom.

Dad gives me a shove. "Go see what he wants."

What have I done now?"

Glossary

adze — an axe with a blade that curves, used for shaping and smoothing wood

auger — a tool used to bore holes

band saw — a power saw with a toothed metal edge used to cut planks

batten — a thin strip of flexible wood

bow — the front of a vessel

broadaxe — a short-handled axe with a broad, flat head

bulwark — where the frames extend above the upper deck to form a solid section

cants — the frames at the bow and the stern

caulking — making watertight by filling the seams with oakum and/or cotton; also, the material used to fill the seams of a vessel

cheeks — the sides of a block of timber bolted below supports for the top of the mast

clamps — the timbers that hold up the deck beams

dubbing — the smoothing of a plank with an adze

frame — an individual rib structure of a vessel

frame up — the raising of a frame and securing it in place

framing stage — a temporary platform or series of platforms around the vessel

futtock — a section of a frame

garboard — the plank next to the keel

graving pieces — small pieces of wood used to fill knotholes in wood

green wood — wood that is unseasoned or not aged

half-model — one half of a scale model of a vessel used as a pattern

head riggings — the system of ropes to support the forward sails, or *head sails*

horn timber — the section of timber extending from the keel to the sternpost

hull — the primary structure of the vessel

keel — the main structure of the vessel to which the frames, stem, and sternpost are attached

lathe — machine used to shape or cut wood or other material

launching — propelling a completed vessel ready for use into the water

milling — cutting or shaping wood with a machine

oakum — tarred rope fibers used for caulking

planks — lengths of wood secured to the sides of the frames and used to construct the deck

preservative — a substance designed to keep wood in an unaltered condition

rabbet — groove cut into the timber in which to place a plank

ribband — a strip of wood used to hold the frames in place while the vessel is being built

schooner — a vessel rigged fore and aft with more than one mast

scrollwork — a fancy design often first etched into the wood with a scroll saw

sheer line — the line where the deck curves

shelf — another support for the deck beams

shore — a support; sometimes used as a verb as in *to support*

spiling — shaping the bow and stern plank edges on the side of the vessel

stanchions — pillars used to support the decks

stations — measurements indicated on the sides and top of a half-model

stem — front support section of the vessel, attached to the keel

stern — the back of the vessel

stern post — a vertical timber attached to the back of the keel

streak — a line of planks from bow to stern; often called strake

trunnel — a wooden nail to fasten timbers; often called tree nail

vessel — a craft designed to carry passengers or cargo on water

waterline — the line on a vessel to which the level of the water rises

watertight — so tightly constructed that water cannot enter

The schooner in my fictional story is an actual vessel, the *Thomas E. Lannon,* that was recently built in the historic Story Boat Yard in Essex, Massachusetts. It was patterned after a 19th-century vessel, the *Nokomis,* one of the last large engine-less schooners to fish off the Grand Banks more than fifty years ago. Built under the direction of Harold Burnham, whose family has been building boats for seven generations, this vessel was designed in the same way as the fastest fishing vessels in the world, with two gaff rigs and headsails. The project was conceived by Thomas Ellis, and the vessel is named for his grandfather, who fished out of the neighboring town of Gloucester during the first half of the past century.

Since I live in Gloucester, I was privileged to record the day-to-day building operations through photographs and to keep a diary much like the boy in my book does. The unique building site along the Essex River, in which 4,000 schooners were built over the years, is now owned and operated by the Essex Shipbuilding Museum, which viewed the raising and sailing of the new schooner as an important part of its educational mission. The entire process called upon the resources not only of the man who envisioned it, and of the designer and builder, but also of those of the descendants of the master builders themselves and of others in the community. Volunteers, including young people, were encouraged to work on the vessel at least one day a week.

Much of the wood, cut down on nearby Hog Island and floated up-river in the time-honored manner of the early ship builders of the region, was milled on site. Though modern equipment such as band saws and planers were needed to achieve a desired result in the shortest space of time, there are some parts of the vessel that required traditional tools. Historically thirty distinct trades were involved in a schooner of this size. With the *Lannon,* problems were solved on an individual basis as the building progressed and as local people with expertise in one area or another came forward.

The *Thomas E. Lannon* is presently berthed at Seven Seas Wharf in Gloucester, Massachusetts, and sets sail for any number of adventures on a regular basis.

ACKNOWLEDGMENTS

I'd like to thank Tom and Kay Ellis, owners of the *Lannon,* for allowing me to visit the shipbuilding site at will and to make a general nuisance of myself. Special appreciation is also due to Harold Burnham, who spent a great deal of time checking my manuscript and storyboard for accuracy and making suggestions.

Writing friends to whom I am indebted for advice include Chris Doyle, Donna McArdle, and Lenice Strohmeier. Thanks, too, to my husband, Wallace, for his continued support of this project as well as for the use of his photograph of the *Lannon* under sail and for the enthusiastic encouragement of my son, Matt Collins, and his wife, Jennifer Mallette.

I'm also grateful to Webster Bull of Commonwealth Editions for seeing the possibilities in the manuscript and photographs, to Jill Feron for her talent in designing the book, to Shawna Mullen for her gentle editorial encouragement and guidance, and to Jay Donahue for his careful editing.

I owe a special debt to author Dana Story, who wrote the books that I consulted for Essex shipbuilding history and to verify my own observations, *Frame-Up!, Growing Up in a Shipyard, Building the Blackfish,* and *The Shipbuilders of Essex.*